W9-AVL-848

SASHI
The Scared Little Sheltie

Linda Greiner

Illustrator
Morgan Spicer

BROWN BOOKS KIDS

This is a work of fiction. Any similarity to real persons, living or dead, is coincidental and not intended by the author.

Sashi, the Scared Little Sheltie

Brown Books Kids
16250 Knoll Trail Drive, Suite 205
Dallas, Texas 75248
www.BrownBooksKids.com
(972) 381-0009

A New Era in Publishing™

ISBN 978-1-61254-214-0
LCCN 2014951612

Printed in the United States
10 9 8 7 6 5 4 3 2 1

For more information or to contact the author, please go to www.NJSheltieMom.com

Dedication

This book is dedicated to
my Sashi, a truly remarkable little dog,
to all Shelties looking for their very own forever
homes, and to the volunteers in Sheltie Rescue
working tirelessly to make these adoptions possible.

Acknowledgments

I would like to thank my family, friends, and coworkers for their support and encouragement. A big shout-out to Morgan Spicer, for bringing Sashi's story to life; Maia, for mentoring and editing; Barbara Kahn and Terry Smith, for their invaluable assistance during Sashi's training; and to Shetland Sheepdog Placement Services of New Jersey, for approving my adoption application, so I could bring our princess home.

Sashi chased everything: cars, bikes, even children. She was herding. She was a Shetland sheepdog—a Sheltie— and that's what she was born to do. When she saw a moving car or children running, she thought of sheep needing to be rounded up and moved into a corral.

Sashi's owners thought she was a bad dog. They didn't understand that she needed to be trained so that she wouldn't run after everything. They scolded her all the time.

They decided they didn't want her any longer and took her to a shelter. Sashi watched as her owners walked away. She didn't know what she had done wrong or why she was there. She was very scared and huddled in the back of her cage.

Visitors came each day to the shelter. The other dogs put their paws up on the front of their cages and barked. "Take me, take me," they seemed to say. No one was interested in Sashi.

She needed help, or she would never be adopted. The shelter manager contacted the Shetland Sheepdog Rescue—a special organization with volunteers who help Shelties find loving families.

9

A lady from the rescue came the next day. Her name was Anita.

"Don't worry," Anita said in a kind voice. "You'll stay with me until we find you a forever home." They left the shelter together.

Sashi was only with Anita for a few days when they had visitors—a mommy and her little girl, Anna. Sashi ran and hid. Suddenly her nose twitched as she caught the scent of something wonderful.

Anna had hot dogs. Sashi was coaxed from hiding and nibbled on pieces of hot dogs.

"We want to adopt you and be your forever family," Anna said.

Anna and her mommy took Sashi home. They had prepared a room with toys and a bed. Sashi tested the bed and decided it was soft, warm, and just the right size. The day's excitement had made her tired. She curled up and fell right to sleep.

Later it was time for a walk. They passed a house with a flag waving in the wind. Sashi barked at the flag. She didn't know what to make of that noisy, flapping thing.

Next they saw a trash can on its side. Sashi barked at that too. She expected something to jump out of the trash can.

There were people across the street walking their dog, and Sashi lunged at them, barking fiercely.

15

It was obvious to Anna's mommy that Sashi hadn't been trained in her first home. Sashi was afraid of everything. Apparently she had never been exposed to the ordinary things that people take for granted. When they got home from their walk, Anna and her mommy started to teach Sashi to "sit" and "check it out."

They practiced every day. When Sashi was afraid of an object, Anna's mommy would tap on it and say, "Check it out." Sashi would approach the scary thing and sniff it. When nothing bad happened, Sashi became calm and stopped barking.

When they were out for a walk and a car or person approached, Anna or her mommy would tell Sashi to sit. She would get a treat and praise when she obeyed.

They worked hard on "sit" and "check it out." As time went on, Sashi wasn't afraid of the things she saw on walks. She sat when she saw cars, bikes, and others with their dogs.

Anna and her mommy also taught Sashi to "come" when she was called. Anna would tell Sashi to sit and then she would walk a few steps away and say, "Sashi, come." Once again, Sashi would get a treat and praise when she obeyed.

As Sashi improved, Anna turned training into a game by hiding somewhere in the house. Then she would call Sashi to come. Sometimes Anna hid behind the bed. Sometimes she hid in the bathtub. Sashi was very good at the game and always found her.

21

One day, mommy took Anna and Sashi to the Sheltie Rescue Picnic. The park was crowded with families and their adopted dogs. There were different contests and games for everyone to play.

23

Anna decided they should try the Sit Contest. They entered an enclosed ring with other people and their dogs. Music played and everyone walked around the ring.

When the music stopped, Anna said, "Sit." Sashi dropped into a sit. The last dog to sit had to leave the ring.

The music started and stopped many times while they walked around the ring. Each time the music stopped, the last Sheltie to sit had to leave. Finally only two were left.

The music started, and almost right away, it stopped. Sashi sat. She was the fastest.

"We won!" Anna shouted in delight. "I'm so proud of you."

Sashi barked as though she was proud too.

Sashi and Anna played for hours with the other dogs. When they got home, they curled up on the sofa and fell sound asleep.

Sashi wasn't a scared little Sheltie anymore. Her new family's love, patience, and training had helped her to become the happy and confident dog she was meant to be.

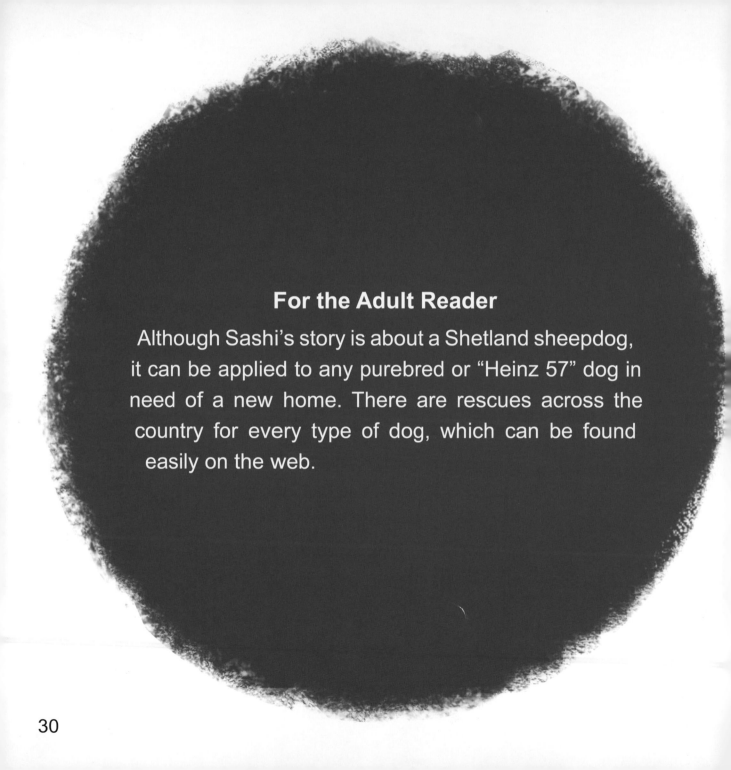

For the Adult Reader

Although Sashi's story is about a Shetland sheepdog, it can be applied to any purebred or "Heinz 57" dog in need of a new home. There are rescues across the country for every type of dog, which can be found easily on the web.

The Shetland Sheepdog

The real Sashi at her first Rescue Picnic.

The Shetland sheepdog, also known as the Sheltie, originated north of Scotland in the Shetland Islands. Known for their sensitive personalities, Shelties love nothing more than to please their owners, and they do best in an environment where gentleness and positive training methods are used.

If you are considering a Sheltie, you could not ask for a more loyal, wonderful companion. Each dog has a distinct personality, but there are basic traits shared by many, if not all, Shelties. They can be quite verbal. They are sound sensitive and often sound reactive, barking at anything from strangers at your door to ringing phones. They can be reserved, so early socialization is needed to keep them from being shy. Shelties are extremely intelligent and very active. They do well in obedience, agility, flyball, herding, and scent detection training. They are bred to work and will often "find a job" if you do not keep them occupied. They are hardwired to chase anything that moves—cars, bikes, birds, or toddlers.

The American Shetland Sheepdog Association has a rescue program with chapters in most states across the country. All rescue dogs are checked by the vet, brought up to date on shots, spayed/neutered, and receive any other medical care appropriate for their situation. Most are fostered in temporary homes, so the dog's personality can be evaluated to ensure the best match in a forever home. Everyone who works in the Sheltie Rescue is a volunteer.

For more information, please visit:
http://www.Assa.org/
http://www.Assa.org/rescue.html

About the Author

Linda Greiner fell in love with Shelties while doing research on what type of dog to get for her sixteenth birthday. Many years later, she decided to adopt a Sheltie instead of buying one from a breeder and contacted the Shetland Sheepdog Placement Services of New Jersey (SSPSNJ). Sashi was her first experience with a severely traumatized dog. With love, patience, positive reinforcement training, and the rescue's support, she was able to overcome Sashi's behavioral problems.

Linda started fostering for SSPSNJ in 2003. Each dog has had a tale to tell. She is currently working on a new book and plans to create a series about Sashi and the rescues she has known and loved. A portion of the proceeds from *Sashi, the Scared Little Sheltie* will benefit Sheltie Rescue.

About the Illustrator

Morgan Spicer is both an animal advocate and an illustrator. Her endless love for animals, especially companion animals, can be seen through her art. She graduated from Syracuse University's BFA program in 2012 and uses her degree to educate children on the benefits of animal companionship. Morgan credits her success to her incredibly supportive family and that includes her nine-year-old blind Shiba Inu, Kiba. She now lives and works in Manhattan with her rescue pup, Roscoe-Roo. Morgan is the Founder of Bark Point Studio and aspires to open her own animal rescue and sanctuary in the future.